ESCAPE FROM
POMPEII

CHRISTINA BALIT

FRANCES LINCOLN CHILDREN'S BOOKS

CHRISTINA BALIT

studied at Chelsea School of Art and the

Royal College of Art. She is also a playwright, and her involvement with

fringe theatre has strongly influenced her illustrative work.

Her first book for Frances Lincoln, Michael Morpurgo's *Blodin the Beast*,

was shortlisted for the 1995 Kate Greenaway Medal and in 1996 *Ishtar and Tammuz*,

written by Christopher Moore, was Commended for the Kate Greenaway Medal.

Among Christina's other books are James Riordan's *The Twelve Labours of Hercules*,

Mary Hoffman's *Women of Camelot* and Robert Leeson's *My Sister Shahrazad*.

Christina is both author and illustrator of *Atlantis: The Legend of a Lost City*.

Her collaboration with Jacqueline Mitton on *Zoo in the Sky: A Book of Animal Constellations*,

won the U.S. Parents' Guide to Children's Media Award, and their next project,

Kingdom of the Sun: A Book of the Planets, was the winner of the

2002 English Association 4-11 Book Award for Key Stage 2 Non-Fiction.

It was followed by *Once Upon a Starry Night* and *Zodiac*.

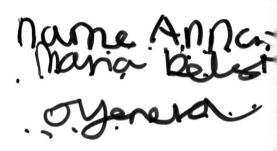

To Mama and Derek
for your boundless grace and courage

Escape from Pompeii copyright © Frances Lincoln Limited 2003
Text and illustrations copyright © Christina Balit 2003

First published in Great Britain in 2003 by Frances Lincoln Children's Books,
4 Torriano Mews, Torriano Avenue, London NW5 2RZ

www.franceslincoln.com

First paperback edition published in 2005

The publishers would like to thank Mavis Nwokobia, Department of Art History
and Archaeology at the University of Manchester, for her help.

British Library Cataloguing in Publication Data
available on request

ISBN 1-84507-059-3

Set in Hiroshige

Printed in Singapore

3 5 7 9 8 6 4

On a hillside overlooking the sparkling bay of Naples, the Roman city of Pompeii glimmered in the sunlight.

From his window, young Tranio listened to the noise humming from bars, taverns and shops around him, and to the busy tradesmen haggling in the streets below. Beyond the massive city walls he could see Pompeii's greatest protector looming in the distance. They called it Vesuvius, the Gentle Mountain.

Could anyone feel safer than here, Tranio wondered? Was anything more beautiful?

Tranio was the son of Dion the actor and lived with his parents near the Theatre District of Pompeii. He'd often sneak to the harbour at the mouth of the River Sarnus and hide behind sacks of grain. There he'd watch pots of wine, oil and spices being carried to and from the ships, or fishermen unloading their rich catches.

Sometimes Tranio went to the forum to watch the politicians make their speeches, the stall-holders argue, and listen to the poets sing.

His favourite song was:

"Rumble down, tumble down,
    great city walls,
Feel the ground grumble,
    the citizens stumble
When the earth shakes, and
    rumble down, tumble down."

Everyone would join in, laughing as they remembered the earthquake tremors. A few years before Tranio was born there had been a big earthquake in Pompeii, and parts of the town had still not yet been fully repaired. But nobody took tremors seriously any more.

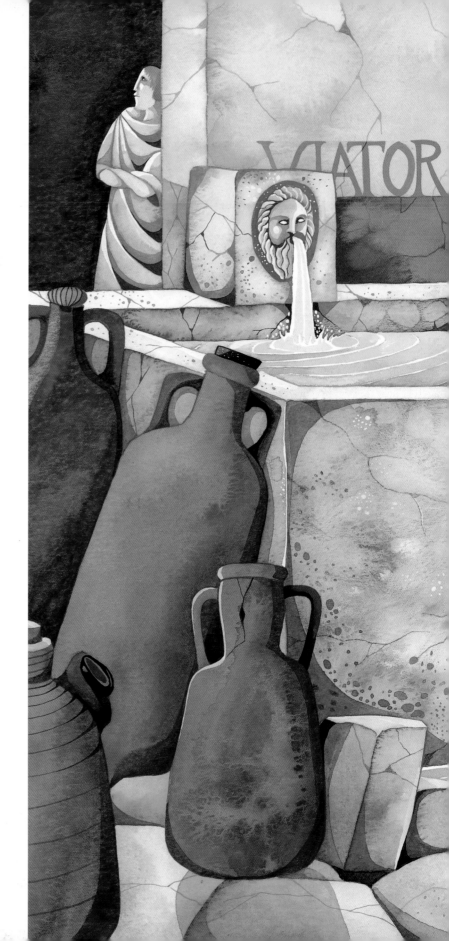

On other mornings, Tranio would shout up to Livia, the baker's daughter, who lived across the street, "Liv! Stop curling your hair and come and play jacks! I've got a bag of bones from mother's kitchen! They're just the right size!"

Livia spent most of her time learning to weave and cook, but during the hot afternoons she and Tranio would squat by the fountain playing knucklebones, or chase dogs down the street.

One hot August day, Dion took Tranio through a shady passage into one of Pompeii's two theatres on the edge of the city, where a pantomime was being rehearsed.

"Sit on the steps, son, and learn!" said Dion. "We'll be using you in small parts soon."

To begin with, Tranio enjoyed watching the sword fights and strutting clowns. The masked actors playing thieves and devils and the leaping acrobats quite took his breath away. But eventually his attention began to wander ...

Then something happened ... The stone steps creaked, the flaps began to rattle and the building quivered. Props fell to the stage and scenery split. Tranio's father froze to the spot. Everyone fell silent.

But one by one the actors began to relax. "Rumble down, tumble down, here we go again!" they chanted.

"Nothing to fear, everybody!" called Tranio's father. "Back to rehearsal, please." The actors fastened their masks and carried on as if nothing had happened.

But Tranio wriggled through the awning and ran away down the street.

He ran as fast as he could to Livia's house. Everyone was shouting, arguing, carrying belongings outside to safety.

"Livia!" he called. "Liv, where are you?" The bakery kitchen was empty. Loaves lay scattered on the floor, the oven blazed and the small donkey turning the corn mill brayed and jumped nervously against its chain.

"Tranio!" Livia leapt down the stairs. "Father's chasing our goat through the market! The poor old thing bolted when the ground began to grumble. You'd have died laughing. Come on!"

Flushed and excited, the two children ran off hand in hand into the dusty streets.

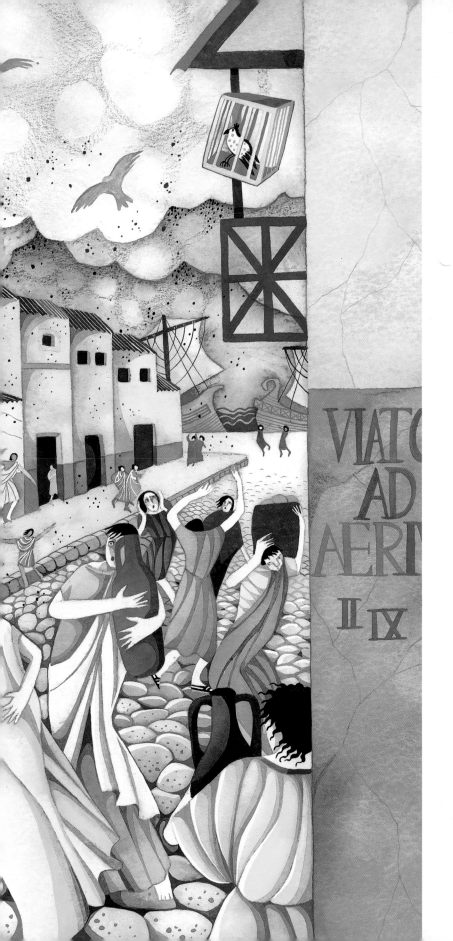

But as they ran, the sky began to darken and a thick cloud drifted slowly overhead.

Livia turned to Tranio. "Why are the seagulls flying towards the woods? They're going the wrong way."

A small bird hanging in a cage chirped frantically, trapped behind its bars, as the air began to fill with ash.

Livia coughed. "Tranio … perhaps we should go back." Tranio grabbed her hand. "We can't go back. The dust is too thick. Quick – the harbour! Run! Just run!"

Boats were bobbing on the choppy water as men began to untie the moorings and ropes. No one noticed two small children climb up the narrow plank of a small Greek cargo ship and hide beneath a pile of coloured rugs. Dusty and tired in their hiding-place, they soon fell asleep.

But as they slept, the anxious captain untied his boat. He sensed that the winds had changed direction, and that the air was uncomfortably hot. The sea began to churn and pull back from the shore.

When Tranio and Livia woke and looked out, they were horrified. Pompeii was getting further and further away. The sky was now thick with pumice and black with ash.

"Tranio, I can't breathe... in the back of my throat..." As she spoke, Livia started to choke. The children could hear dogs barking and people's muffled screams as they ran gasping for air with rags covering their mouths or pillows over their heads, some falling to the grumbling, trembling ground.

And then, in one terrible endless moment, they heard mighty Mount Vesuvius roar. Its top exploded in a scream and flames ripped upwards to the sky. A massive cloud of silver ash rose to the heavens, twisting and bubbling in every direction until everything was in total darkness.

Lightning flashed and thunder roared. Streams of molten liquid flowed in fast rivers down the mountain slopes and covered a nearby town. The walls, streets and gardens of their beloved Pompeii disappeared beneath a blanket of ash and stones. Before their very eyes, everything and everyone they had ever loved was destroyed.

Tranio and Livia held each other desperately as the steaming lava reached the sea itself. The water began to swell against the sides of the boat as it moved slowly out to safety.

They had left just in time. Soon the sea sank back from the shore and even the fishes were stranded there.

Many years passed ... and the mountain grew cool and still. At first its slopes were burnt and barren, but in time plants began to grow as the volcanic soil brought forth its riches once more. Most people had forgotten the buried city.

An old man and woman stood in the shade of an orange tree and laid a flower there. Long ago, they had been rescued by the kind captain of a Greek cargo ship and he had raised them as his own. They were Tranio and Livia, saying farewell to those buried under the ash beneath their feet.

"We won't forget you," they whispered.

Would anyone ever find their beloved Pompeii, they wondered? Would anyone ever see its splendid streets? Perhaps. Perhaps not.

Tranio and Livia walked back to their small house beside the orange grove. For the rest of their days they would carry a deep sorrow within their hearts.

The Story of Pompeii

Before the eruption of Mount Vesuvius, Pompeii was a busy, beautiful Roman city where about 15,000 people lived. In those days Vesuvius appeared green and peaceful, but on 24 August in AD 79, a great mushroom-shaped cloud rose from its top and, to everyone's surprise, the volcano began to erupt. In nearby Pompeii, day became as dark as night. Showers of ash and stones fell and began to cover streets and houses. Within a few hours rooftops started to collapse, and many people fled. The next morning, clouds of poisonous gases and ash poured down from the volcano, suffocating those who had stayed behind.

When the dust had settled, Pompeii and its lovely surroundings had disappeared beneath a blanket of ash, pumice-stone and lava. The city had become like the Sleeping Beauty's castle. Trees and plants grew over it and although, as time passed, people remembered the city of Pompeii, they forgot exactly where it had been. Pompeii slept for nearly 1,700 years, until, in 1748, excavators began to find its remains. Temples, theatres, baths, shops and beautifully-painted houses were uncovered, along with skeletons of the victims, sometimes in family groups. Soon Pompeii became famous and people came from far and wide to see it. They were amazed at what they saw.

In 1863 the archaeologist Guiseppe Fiorelli decided to try an experiment. He noticed that where a body had lain in the ash, it had left hollows in the shape of the body that had once been there. He poured plaster into one body space and waited for it to set. When the ashes around it were removed, he found that he was left with a plaster cast in the exact shape of the victim's body. Since then, many casts have been made and can be seen in Pompeii – sad reminders of the city's fate.

Vesuvius has not erupted since March 1944, but the volcano is not dead – only sleeping. Like all volcanoes, it has given the land around it rich soil which is easy to farm. Just as in Roman times, people have built their homes there and towns and villages crowd the shores of the Bay of Naples. One day Vesuvius will erupt again, but now, with modern scientific instruments checking the volcano each day, it is hoped that that no more lives will be lost.

Pompeii is not yet fully excavated, but its uncovered remains help us see what a Roman city really looked like, and how the Romans lived, worked and played.

NEAPOLIS

ROME

POMPEII

MEDITERRANEAN SEA

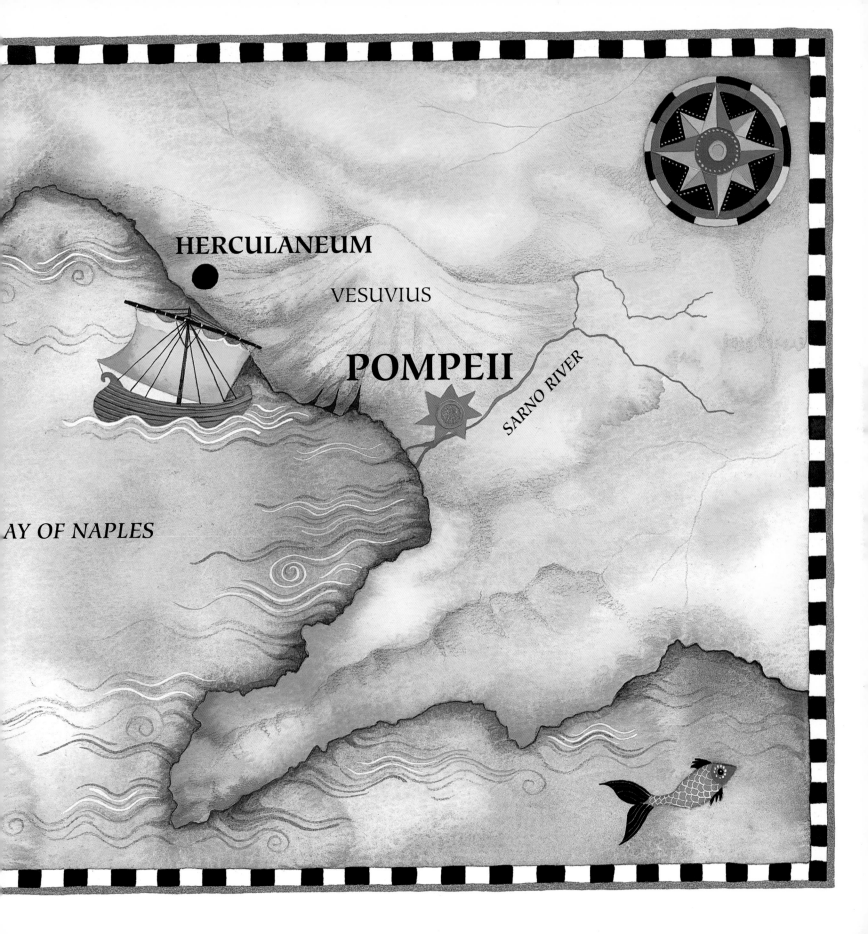

HERCULANEUM

VESUVIUS

POMPEII

SARNO RIVER

AY OF NAPLES

Atlantis
The Legend of a Lost City
Christina Balit

Floating on the emerald seas is a small rocky island
belonging to the mighty sea-god Poseidon.
When Poseidon marries an islander named Cleito he transforms
Atlantis into a rich and fertile place, with a palace fit for a god.
But as the years pass, his descendants start to act less
like gods and more like men...

ISBN 0-7112-1906-0

The Twelve Labours of Hercules
James Riordan
Illustrated by Christina Balit

Stronger than a lion, wiser than the stars, protector of gods and men...
Here, in a spirited retelling, are the life and labours
of mythology's mightiest warrior-hero, Hercules! Christina Balit's
powerful illustrations help to make this a heroic anthology
that children will reach for again and again.

ISBN 0-7112-1391-7

My Sister Shahrazad
Tales from the One Thousand and One Nights
Robert Leeson
Illustrated by Christina Balit

When the king of Baghdad's wife betrays him,
he trusts no woman. But brave Shahrazad has a plan.
Offering herself as a bride, she resolves to spend
each night telling the king a story and
thereby to win his heart.

ISBN 0-7112-1767-X

Frances Lincoln titles are available from all good bookshops.
You can also buy books and find out more about your favourite titles, authors and illustrators
on our website: www.franceslincoln.com